Little Scraggly Hair
A Dog on Noah's Ark

by LYNN CULLEN

illustrated by JACQUELINE ROGERS

Holiday House / New York

AUTHOR'S NOTE

The legend of how the dog got a wet nose first appears in print as "The 'Ole in the Ark," by Marriott Edgar, a Scottish writer and stage performer. This poem was found in the monologue collection *Albert and Balbus and Samuel Small* (EMI Music Publishing Ltd., 1937). "The 'Ole in the Ark" was later performed by Stanley Holloway, an English actor and storyteller, and can be found in his audio recording *The Classic Monologues* (Avid, 2000). The story can also be found on video in a recording done in 1986 by Irish-born Maggi Peirce in the *American Storytelling Series, Volume One* (Wilson Video Resource Collection). All of these versions focus on Noah and his gratitude to the dog for plugging the hole in the ark. In contrast I retold the story from the dog's point of view, emphasizing the development of the dog's long-standing friendship with humankind. After finding a brief version of the tale in *The Child's Book of Folklore* (Dial Press, 1947), a collection of American lore edited by Marion Vallat Emrich and George Korson, I also took the liberty of setting the story in America. To do so, I chose the uniquely American speech of southern Appalachia as recorded in the 1950s by eminent folklorist Richard Chase in his book *American Folk Tales and Songs* (Dover Publications, 1956). By using this dialect in *Little Scraggly Hair*, I hoped to preserve a voice that is a valuable part of our national heritage.

Text copyright © 2003 by Lynn Cullen

Illustrations copyright © 2003 by Jacqueline Rogers

All Rights Reserved

The medium for the artwork was watercolor.

The text typeface is Aunt Mildred.

Printed in the United States of America

www.holidayhouse.com

First Edition

Library of Congress Cataloging-in-Publication Data

Cullen, Lynn.

Little Scraggly Hair: a dog on Noah's ark / by Lynn Cullen ; illustrated by Jacqueline Rogers—1st ed.

p. cm.

Summary: At a time when men and dogs are not friendly, Scraggly Hair helps Noah build an ark

and round up the pairs of animals it will carry, but conditions on the boat

turn his warm, dry nose to a cold, wet one.

ISBN 0-8234-1772-7 (hardcover)

1. Dogs—Juvenile fiction. [1.Dogs—Fiction. 2. Noah's ark—Fiction.

3. Noah (Biblical figure)—Fiction. 4. Deluge—Fiction.] I. Rogers, Jacqueline, ill. II. Title.

PZ10.3.C8975Li 2003

[E]—dc21

2002192203

For Carol Price, who planted the seed,
and Barbara Kouts, who kept it growing
—L. C.

For Martha
—J. R.

Way, way back, long before your great-granddaddy's time, dogs had warm, dry noses. Blame if they didn't stick 'em everywhere—sniffin', snortin', snitchin' table scraps. Now in them days, folks didn't take much to dogs. Thought dogs were no count, just toters of fleas, lickers of fry pans. Sure wouldn't let 'em in their cabins. Sooner ask in their pigs.

Now dogs didn't take much to humans neither. They just wanted to mosey 'round with the other dogs, diggin' up bones and chasin' cats.

But here comes this one little dog, a little scraggly-haired feller. He ain't much for diggin' up bones. Ain't much for bedevilin' cats, either. Truth is, he's partial to 'em. Likes the way they purr.

Well, the other dogs don't favor that. Say, "Git on out, Scraggly Hair. Go play with your cats." So *snip, snap, snout*, they turn him right out.

But the cats don't want him neither. Don't trust his kind a'tall. Reckon first chance he gets, he'll scare 'em up a tree. So *scritch, scratch, scruff*, they grab him by the ruff. Send Little Scraggly Hair dustin' down the road.

Ain't no time 'til his belly gets sore—can't find a bite to eat. And from all that wanderin', his paws get cut up, too. But that ain't nothin' compared to the pain in his heart. That little dog is powerful lonely.

Then one day Little Scraggly Hair limps into a barnyard where there's this feller a-sawin' and a-hammerin' away. Now in them days, folks were bad ornery to each other, fightin' and cussin' and carryin' on, but they were extra ornery to dogs. Well, Little Scraggly Hair's paws are cut up fierce. He's just about starved. So he sinks right down in the dirt. Reckons he'll rest 'til he gets chased off.

But the man just keeps a-sawin' and a-hammerin'. Seems he's buildin' a boat—only there ain't no water for miles around, just cornfields far as meets the eye. The boat's big, too. Bigger 'n twenty, thirty cabins. Keeps the man busy—don't even see Little Scraggly Hair. Don't look up 'til dusk, when his young'un brings him an ash cake. Then the man sits down on a log, but he's so give out from hammerin', he can hardly eat.

Well, Little Scraggly Hair knows better 'n to beg. He's all scrinched up, ready to scoot, when the man sees him. The man raises his hand, r'ars back . . .

. . . and throws the dog a crumb.

Little Scraggly Hair don't know what to do. Ain't no one's ever been good to him before. He wants to thank the man. So before he takes the crumb, he does the only thing he can figure—gives the man a nudge with his warm, dry nose.

A smile kinks up the corners of the man's mouth. He looks at his ash cake, then at the dog. The next thing you know, 'tween the two of 'em, *slip, slap, slurp,* nothin's left but a burp.

From then on, Little Scraggly Hair follows the feller like a calf. He fetches him bits of wood. Totes his bag of nails. Come evening, the man shares his bite of supper. Little Scraggly Hair gives him a nudge with his warm, dry nose.

Then one day the neighbors stop by. "What you buildin' there, Noah?" they ask the man.

"It's an ark," says Noah.

"You can call it what you want," they say. "Looks like a boat. What you goin' to do—sail through your cornfield?"

"No, sir," says Noah. "God told me to git me two of every critter alive and put 'em onboard. Says a big flood's a-comin'."

The neighbors r'ar back, laughin'. "A flood! You lost your sense? And how in the nation you goin' to round up all them critters?"

"Don't know," says Noah.

"And what's that dog doin' hangin' 'round? He'll put fleas in your feather bed. Muss up the hookrug. Shoo, dog! Shoo!"

Noah stops 'em. "Let him be."

The neighbors just shake their heads. Say Ole Noah's gone crazy. Buildin' arks. Keepin' dogs.

Noah's young'uns, they're sore ashamed. When it's time to gather up
the critters, don't none of 'em do a lick of work. "Can't," they say. "Too
tuckered."

"Too riled."

"Got a hangnail."

Noah knows better 'n to ask his wife. With the neighbors a-chortlin'
and her young'uns a-blubberin', she's as mad as a wet cat.

Only one creature is willin' to help. Little Scraggly Hair.
Just like he was born to it, he herds them critters into the ark,
dodgin' elephants' feet and crocodiles' teeth. He knows to be
tough on the tigers but tender on the mice.

Two of every critter is a powerful big herd. The dog is still roundin' 'em up when rain busts out. The water's clean up to his chest before Noah yells, "Git on up here, dog!"

Little Scraggly Hair bounds up the ramp, but there's no more room. He's stuck 'tween a pair of cranky bears and two snortin' buffalos. Fit's so tight, he has to stick his nose through a knothole.

And so it goes for forty days. Forty days of cold, hard rain patterin' down on the dog's nose. Forty days of bein' crushed between the bears and the buffalos.

Forty days of nothin' to eat unless a fish jumps.

Things ain't much better for Noah.

"Daddy, when we gettin' off this ark?" say the young'uns.

"Brother's pullin' my hair."

"Sister's spittin' in my stew."

Noah's wife, she's havin' a fit. All the brayin' and yappin' and roarin' of the critters has give her a headache. "Noah," she says, "wherever we're goin', we had better git there quick."

Just then his littlest girl calls out, "Look here, Daddy. That scraggly-haired dog of your'n—there's something on his nose."

They all look. Sure enough, there on the dog's wet nose sits a mourny dove, an olive branch in its beak.

"If they's branches, they's trees," says Noah. "And where they's trees, they's land."

"Hallelujah!" yell the young'uns.

"It's about time," says his wife.

Soon enough, they're back on land. All the critters find themselves
new homes. Noah builds himself a cabin. Finally makes himself a fire.
Then he sees Little Scraggly Hair, still hangin' 'round.

"Thank ye," he says to the dog. "I suppose you want to git now, find yourself a better life." He bends down to give Little Scraggly Hair one last pat. It's then he sees the dog's nose is as cold and wet as a creek bottom.

"Now that won't do," says Noah. "Have to warm you in front of the fire." He looks guiltylike at his wife. "It'll only be the night," he says. "Just 'til his nose is done dry."

Then, pure gentle, like the mist risin'
soft from the land, Little Scraggly Hair
lays his head on Noah's feet. And *hish,
hush, heap*, that dog falls clean asleep.

Try as he might, Noah can't get that dog's nose dry. It's as cold and wet as it was on the ark. "Won't be much longer," Noah tells his wife. He don't say nothin' when his littlest girl totes a pup she found to the fire. "One more can't hurt, can it, Daddy?"

Well, Little Scraggly Hair's nose never did warm up and dry off. Sure enough, all their pups that came after 'em had cold, wet noses, too— fact, all dogs do to this very day. Folks still keep their dogs by their fires, sharin' their bits of supper, givin' 'em little pats. Seems it's always been that a-way.

Reckon it's not a-changin' anytime soon.